Little Bear's Trousers

For my Mother – in her memory

A Red Fox Book

Published by Random House Children's Books
20 Vauxhall Bridge Road, London SW1V 2SA

A division of Random House UK Ltd
London Melbourne Sydney Auckland
Johannesburg and agencies throughout the world

1 3 5 7 9 10 8 6 4 2

First published by Hutchinson Children's Books 1987
Red Fox edition 1988

This Red Fox mini edition 1994

Printed in China
RANDOM HOUSE UK Limited Reg. No. 954009
ISBN 0 09 922931 5

JANE HISSEY

Little Bear's Trousers

RED FOX

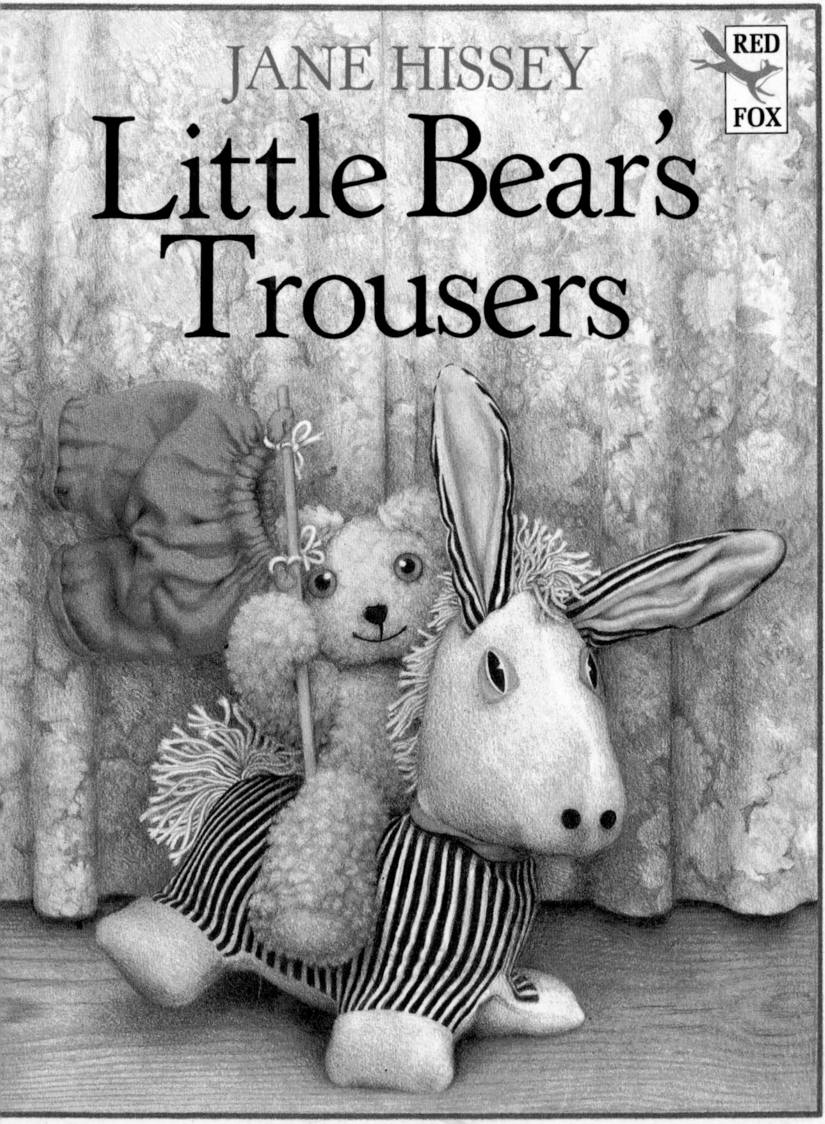

JANE HISSEY

Little Bear's Trousers

RED FOX

THE sun shone through the window and woke Little Bear. 'What a lovely morning,' he said to himself. 'I'll do something different today.'

OLD Bear was already enjoying the sun in his deckchair. 'I haven't seen your trousers, I'm afraid,' he said. 'But Camel was around here earlier. Perhaps she knows where they are.'

'OH dear,' said Camel, when Little Bear found her a few minutes later. 'I did find them. I thought they were a pair of hump warmers and I tried them on to see if they fitted me. They did keep my humps *quite* warm but the air came down the tops so I decided these were better.' And she showed Little Bear two very smart bobble hats – one for each hump.

'I gave the old hump warmers to Sailor to use as sails for his boat. Jump on my back and let's see if we can find him.' Little Bear scrambled up and they galloped off in the direction of the bathroom.

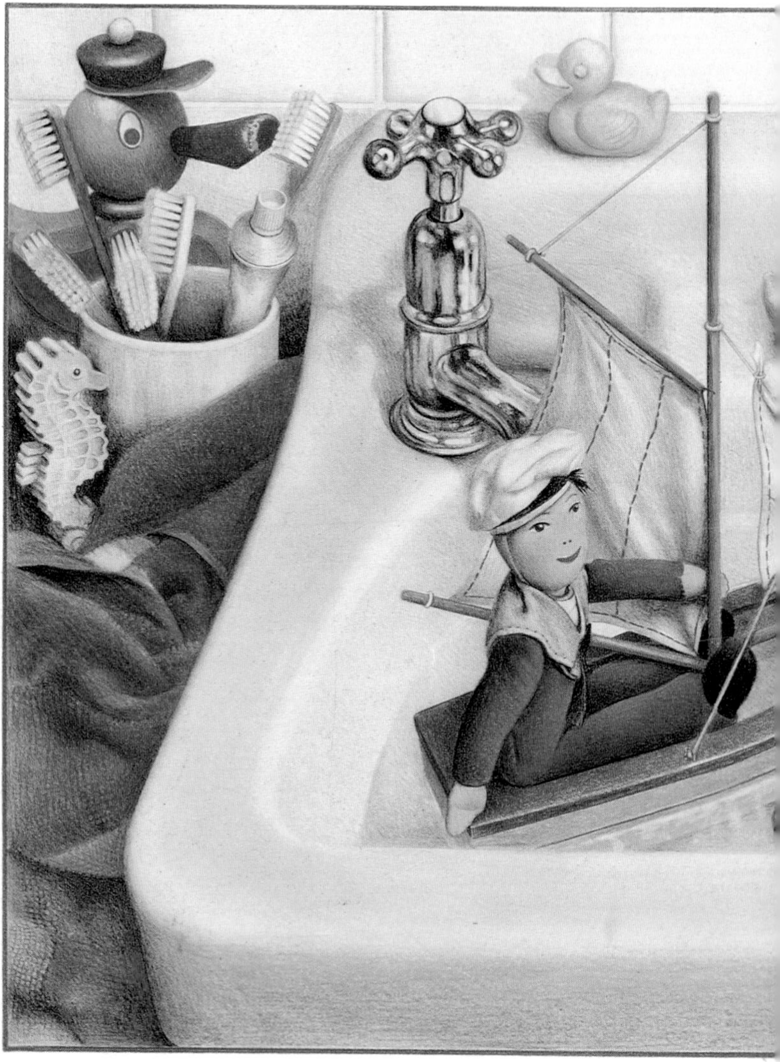

DOG was happily burying his bones in flowerpots when Little Bear found him. 'My bones kept falling through the two-bone bone-holder,' he said.

'TWO-BONE BONE-HOLDER!' cried Little Bear in dismay. 'Oh, Dog, can't you recognize trousers when you see them?'

'Oh, dear,' said Dog. 'I do feel silly. I gave them to Rabbit – he said he needed a skiing hat, and your trousers looked just perfect. I am sorry.'

ZEBRA was building herself a house when Little Bear arrived. But his trousers were nowhere to be seen.

'I wondered whose they were,' she said. 'They were terribly useful. I tied up the legs with string, put them on my back and carried all these bricks here in them. But when I had enough bricks for my house I gave them to Duck to use as a flag for his sand castle. I am sorry, Little Bear. I didn't know they belonged to you.'

DUCK was in the sand tray looking sadly at the castle he'd made. There was no trouser flag on the top now. 'I did use the flag that Zebra gave me,' he sighed. 'But Bramwell Brown came and said it was just what he needed, urgently, in the kitchen. He gave me this paper flag to use instead.'

'Never mind,' said Little Bear with a sigh, feeling quite glad that his trousers were not covered in sand.

The kitchen was in a terrible muddle. There were bowls and spoons and eggs and flour, and in the middle of it all sat Bramwell Brown.

HE had Little Bear's trousers but, oh dear, he'd filled them with pink icing and was busy decorating a huge cake with them.

'It's a special occasion cake,' said Bramwell. 'And you have to put icing on special occasion cakes. I thought I could do two stripes at once with these icing bags.'

'But they're *not* icing bags. They are my trousers!' sniffed Little Bear, trying hard not to cry.

'I thought I'd seen them before,' said Bramwell Brown.

DUCK washed Little Bear's trousers and dried them next to the cooker. Then all the toys sat down to enjoy a piece of cake and to celebrate the day Little Bear lost, and found, his trousers.

AND ever since Trousers Day, Little Bear has slept with his trousers under his pillow. 'Nobody will find them there,' he says.

A RED FOX PICTURE BOOK

Little Bear has lost his trousers. Where *can* they be? All the toys have seen them and used them in some very un-trousery ways. But no-one can tell Little Bear where his trousers are now!

The second delightful Old Bear story by Jane Hissey.

"Delicious and extraordinary"
PUBLISHING NEWS

ISBN 0-09-922931-
9 780099 229315
UK £1.99 CAN $3.95